Oh, A-Hunting We Will Go

story by John Langstaff

pictures by Nancy Winslow Parker

 **D.C. Heath and Company**
Lexington, Massachusetts / Toronto, Ontario

Acknowledgments

Grateful acknowledgment is made for permission to reprint the following copyrighted material.

OH, A-HUNTING WE WILL GO, by John Langstaff and illustrated by Nancy Winslow Parker. Copyright © 1974 by John Langstaff and Nancy Winslow Parker. This edition is reprinted by arrangement with Macmillan Publishing Company, a division of Macmillan, Inc.

Cover Design: Studio Goodwin-Sturges. Calligraphy: Colleen.

Editorial Permissions: Dorothy McLeod.

Design Series: Leslie Dews. Kindergarten Program: Trelawney Goodell. Book: Dianne Cassidy.

Production Carol Lanza.

Oh,
A-Hunting
We Will Go

Oh, a-hunting we will go,

A-hunting we will go;

We'll catch a fox

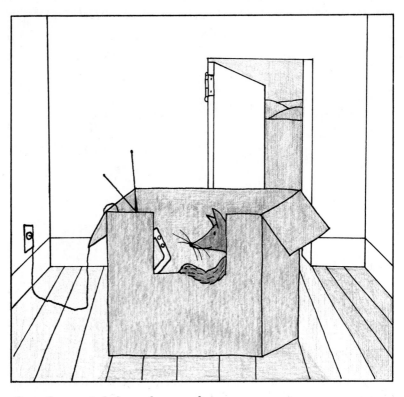

And put him in a box,

And then we'll let him go!

Oh, a-hunting we will go,

A-hunting we will go;

We'll catch a lamb

And put him in a pram,

And then we'll let him go!

Oh, a-hunting we will go,

A-hunting we will go;

We'll catch a goat

And put him in a boat,

And then we'll let him go!

Oh, a-hunting we will go,

A-hunting we will go;

We'll catch a bear

And put him in underwear,

And then we'll let him go!

Oh, a-hunting we will go,
   A-hunting we will go;
We'll catch a whale

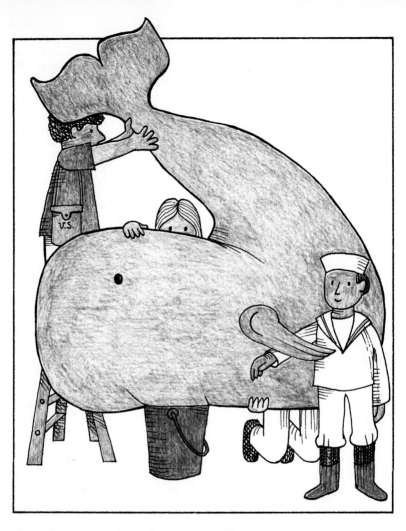

And put him in a pail,

And then we'll let him go!

14

Oh, a-hunting we will go,

   A-hunting we will go;

We'll catch a snake

And put him in a cake,

And then we'll let him go!

Oh, a-hunting we will go,
A-hunting we will go;
We'll catch a mouse

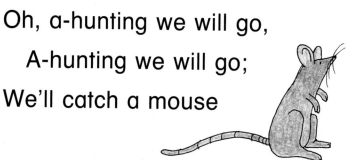

And put him in a house,

And then we'll let him go!

Oh, a-hunting we will go,

A-hunting we will go;

We'll catch a pig

And put him in a wig,

And then we'll let him go!

Oh, a-hunting we will go,

A-hunting we will go;

We'll catch a skunk

And put him in a bunk,

And then we'll let him go!

Oh, a-hunting we will go,

A-hunting we will go;

We'll catch an armadillo

And put him in a pillow,

And then we'll let him go!

Oh, a-hunting we will go,

A-hunting we will go;

We'll catch a fish

And put him in a dish,

And then we'll let him go!

Oh, a-hunting we will go,

A-hunting we will go;

We'll catch a brontosaurus

And put him in a chorus,

And then we'll let him go!

Oh, a-hunting we will go,
  A-hunting we will go;
We'll catch an ape

And put him in a cape,

And then we'll let him go!

Oh, a-hunting we will go,
 A-hunting we will go;
We'll just pretend and in the end,
 We'll always let them go!

Oh, A-Hunting We Will Go

Oh, a-hunting we will go, A-hunting we will go; We'll catch a fox and put him in a box, And then we'll let him go!

We'll catch a lamb and put him in a pram,
  And then we'll let him go!

We'll catch a goat and put him in a boat,
  And then we'll let him go!

We'll catch a bear and put him in underwear
  And then we'll let him go!

We'll catch a whale and put him in a pail,
  And then we'll let him go!

We'll catch a snake and put him in a cake,
  And then we'll let him go!

We'll catch a mouse and put him in a house,
  And then we'll let him go!

We'll catch a pig and put him in a wig,
  And then we'll let him go!

We'll catch a skunk and put him in a bunk,
  And then we'll let him go!

We'll catch an armadillo and put him in a pillow,
  And then we'll let him go!

We'll catch a fish and put him in a dish,
  And then we'll let him go!

We'll catch a brontosaurus and put him in a chorus,
  And then we'll let him go!

We'll catch an ape and put him in a cape,
  And then we'll let him go!

  We'll just pretend and in the end,
  We'll always let them go!